IAL CRITTER

WITHDRAWN

BY GINA AND MERCER MAYER

For Caroline Hall

A Random House PICTUREBACK® Book

Random House 🏠 New York

A Very Special Critter book, characters, text, and images copyright © 1992 Gina and Mercer Mayer.
Little Critter, Mercer Mayer's Little Critter, and Mercer Mayer's Little Critter and Logo are registered trademarks and Little Critter Classics
and Logo is a trademark of Orchard House Licensing Company. All rights reserved. No part of this book may be reproduced or copied in any
form without written permission from the copyright owner. Published in the United States by Random House Children's Books, a division of
Penguin Random House LLC, 1745 Broadway, New York, NY 10019, and in Canada by Penguin Random House Canada Limited, Toronto.
Originally published in slightly different form by Golden Books, an imprint of Random House Children's Books, New York, in 1992.
Pictureback, Random House, and the Random House colophon are registered trademarks of Penguin Random House LLC.

Visit us on the Web!
rhcbooks.com
littlecritter.com

Educators and librarians, for a variety of teaching tools, visit us at RHTeachersLibrarians.com

ISBN 978-1-9848-3075-3 (trade) — ISBN 978-1-9848-3076-0 (ebook)

MANUFACTURED IN CHINA
10 9 8 7 6 5 4 3 2 1

Random House Children's Books supports the First Amendment and celebrates the right to read.

One day my teacher said, "A new critter is coming to our class tomorrow."

I was glad. I hoped the new critter would be someone really cool.

Then my teacher said, "Our new student is a very special critter. He can't walk, so he uses a wheelchair. I want you all to try very hard to make him feel at home."

I was a little scared because I had never known anyone in a wheelchair before.

I told my dad about it. He said, "Just because he's in a wheelchair doesn't mean he's any different than the rest of you. He probably just needs some special help once in a while."

I thought that made sense.

The next day they brought the new student to our class.
He looked scared.

But his wheelchair was really cool. It had stickers of dinosaurs and funny monsters all over it.

My teacher said, "This is our new student. Alex, we are very happy to have you in our class."

Then we all introduced ourselves.

I was curious about Alex. So was everyone else. At recess we all talked to Alex. Some critters asked him questions about his wheelchair.
He didn't seem to mind.

At first everyone in the class thought
Alex needed a lot of help.

We were wrong.

He can go almost anywhere he wants
in his wheelchair. Once in a while he needs
a little push to get over a bump.

His wheelchair can't go up stairs, so he
rolls it up the special ramp at school.

His wheelchair has pouches to carry his books
and things he needs for school. Sometimes he
even carries *my* books for me.

Sometimes Alex needs help reaching things way up high. Sometimes I do, too.

He plays games in the playground with the rest of us. When we play dodgeball, he always gets the most people out.

And he's great at volleyball.

He does have a little trouble
with hide-and-seek, though.

Alex rides a special bus. It has a lift that takes his wheelchair up and down.

We take turns helping him to the bus.

Alex likes the same things my other
friends like. He plays with race cars and
dinosaurs, and he loves Super Critter.

For our Halloween party at school,
Alex dressed up like a car. He had the
best costume in the whole school.

He's a good artist, too. He won
an art contest at school and our
class got an ice cream party.

Once in a while something will come up that Alex needs help with.

250
X5
1250

But it's no big deal. Sometimes I need him to help me, too.

My dad was right about Alex.
Even though he's a special critter,
he's just one of the gang.